For our little sloth.

Deep in the jungle, at the top of one of the tallest trees, there is a small but cozy tree house. This tree house is the home of a curious little sloth named Pocket.

Pocket isn't just any normal sloth.
He has a knack for solving mysteries,
so his friends call him a "Sloth Sleuth".

Pocket's pen pals are known to write
him letters to help solve mysteries.

"Oh look, Owl! Another letter from a friend!"
said Pocket.

"Who? Who?" responded Owl,
his friendly neighbor.

It was a letter from Pocket's friend Winston
in London, writing that the Queen's most
prized possessions had gone missing.

"Time to pack my suitcase!"
Pocket exclaimed.

Pocket loved visiting his friends, partially
because he enjoyed the nice long naps
he could take along the way.

When Pocket's plane landed in England,
Winston was waiting outside Heathrow airport.

"Pocket, I'm so glad you're here!" Winston cried.
"We have to find the Queen's treasures
before she returns!"

"Happy to help!" Pocket said. "What exactly are
we looking for? Crown Jewels? Gold bars?"

"No!" Winston said, anxiously.
"Her pet corgis have gone missing!"

Pocket knew right away that this
was a *very* important case.

Pocket and Winston stood in front of
Buckingham Palace, home to the Queen
and the Royal Family.

Winston explained that this was the last place
the corgis were seen. They had been out
for their walk, and just disappeared.

Pocket thought this was strange indeed,
and wanted to get to higher ground for
a better view of the city.

Luckily, Winston knew just the spot.

The pair boarded a carriage on a
large Ferris wheel called the London Eye.
Sitting on the bank of the Thames River,
Pocket knew this would be the perfect
spot to see all of London.

From up high, Pocket was able to spot
landmarks he saw on his map, including Big Ben,
St. Paul's Cathedral, and Tower Bridge.

But... no corgis.

As they were leaving, they passed by photos of tourists in the souvenir shop. One picture in particular caught Pocket's eye.

"Look Winston!" Pocket exclaimed. "The corgis!"

"By golly, you're right!" Winston cried. "And what's that they have with them?"

Using his magnifying glass, Pocket looked closer at the picture. It was a map of London, and it had St. Paul's Cathedral circled. Pocket knew this was a clue!

Pocket and Winston decided the fastest way to get to the church was to take the London Underground, also known as the Tube.

On the way, Pocket started to mark their journey on his map. He loved a good adventure!

As Pocket and Winston exited the Tube station, they saw a large, white cathedral in front of them. Pocket was in awe of such a beautiful building, and wouldn't blame the corgis if they came sight-seeing here.

The pair started walking around the church looking for more clues.

Pocket ducked between the tourists and
entertainers in the square. He walked by a
caricaturist, a special kind of artist, and saw
a picture of a funny looking group of dogs.

"Winston, you've got to see this!"
Pocket shouted.

"By George, it's the pups!"
Winston said.

Pocket took a closer look at the picture, and saw that the corgis were dressed in strange, old clothing.

After giving it some thought, he realized that the dogs were dressed like Shakespearean characters.

"Maybe the corgis were thinking about seeing a play?" Pocket asked Winston.

"Well, then," Winston said, "I know just the place to see a Shakespearean play in London!"

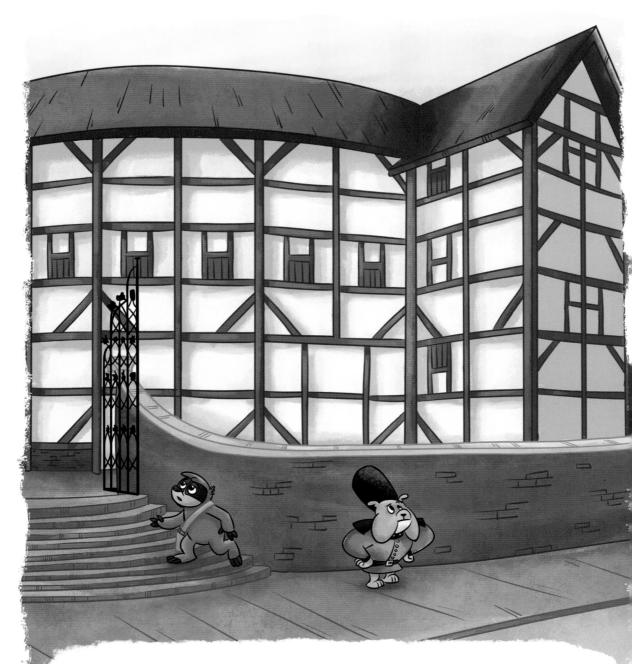

Winston guided Pocket to the Globe Theater, where William Shakespeare would have actors perform his most famous plays.

Pocket started exploring around the old building, hoping that the corgis left a clue here, too.

"Pocket, I've found something!"
Winston shouted.

Winston was sniffing at a pamphlet for Big Ben
that was covered in puppy paw prints.

"This has got to be where the pooches are,"
Pocket said. "On to our next stop!"

Pocket and Winston got back on the Tube and headed toward Big Ben and Westminster Abbey.

When they arrived at the tower, Pocket marveled at the sight.

"No time to dawdle," Winston said. "We've got to find those puppies."

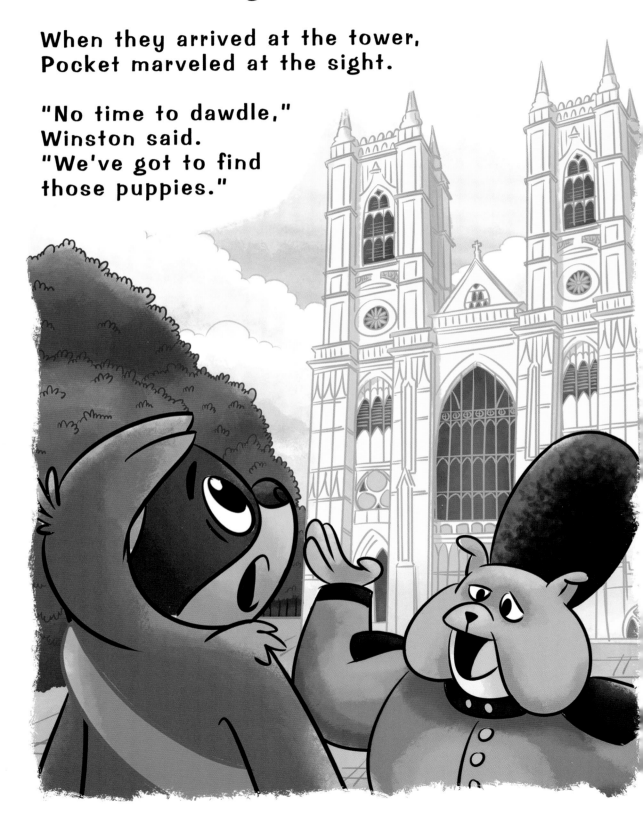

Pocket recommended that they split up
and search for the corgis; that way
they could cover more ground.

Pocket and Winston started
exploring the area, looking
for any sign of the dogs.

Big Ben started chiming, filling the square
with noise. Then, a small group of dogs
started barking along with the ringing.

"The corgis!" Pocket cried. "We found them!"

Winston let out a loud yelp. "We were worried
sick about you chaps!" he scolded.

Apologizing, the corgis went on to explain how every
day they took the same walk, and had just wanted
to explore a bit more. Next thing they knew,
they were lost!

"Not to worry. We'll help you find your
way home," Pocket said reassuringly.

The group arrived back at Buckingham Palace
in the nick of time. The Queen's car was
just pulling into the driveway.

The Queen was overjoyed to be
welcomed home by her precious dogs.

"And who is your friend?" the Queen asked.

Pocket was nervous! He had never
met a queen before.

"My name is Pocket," he squeaked.
"I suppose I'm your corgis' tour guide!"

"From what I understand, you're more
than that!" the Queen exclaimed.
"I heard my most precious pups disappeared,
and that you brought them home."

"Well," Pocket blushed. "All in a day's work,
Your Majesty."

The Queen could think of only one way to
properly thank Pocket. She asked the little sloth
to kneel so that she could knight him.

Pocket was bursting with pride at the honor.

"Thank you for your service,
Sir Pocket!"

The next day, before Pocket left for the airport, he joined the corgis and Winston for their daily walk. The pups were overjoyed to be exploring a new spot, and Hyde Park offered a lot of bushes and trees to play around.

As Pocket made the climb up to his tree house, he was looking forward to a good night's sleep after his adventures across the pond.

Pocket drifted off to sleep, dreaming
about where his next adventure would be.